ASHES
OF THE
WORLD

THE WORLD BURNS - BOOK 2

BOYD CRAVEN

TABLE OF CONTENTS

CHAPTER 1

Do you think there's going to be any more raiders?" asked Lisa.

"Everyone we found out there was dead. How many were in that group?" Blake asked.

"You know, I never really got a good look at everyone," said Weston.

"Yeah, we spent most of our time avoiding people. Things in town got absolutely crazy after that EMP," said Bobby.

"That's what I don't understand. You guys keep saying EMP. How do you know for sure that's what actually happened?" Sandra asked them.

"Weston called me. He said that the police department had gotten an alert. He was rushing home when one of the bombs went off in space," Lisa said, looking back and forth between both of her sons for confirmation.

"Yes, that part was really scary. It was like a dream. Or a nightmare."

"When Weston called me, I thought he was kidding, but I was close to Mom's house anyway, so I went over there to check on things when the lights went out," said Bobby.

"So are we at war? Are we being invaded? Who did this to us?" Blake asked.

"I don't know," Weston said. "The news on the radio, well, you know it's all rumor, but they think it was Iran working with ISIS. They think the missiles were launched off of freighters. The last I heard, the ships that launched the missiles were sunk."

"What do you mean the ships? Plural, more than one?" Duncan said, his voice worried.

"There was a launch on Virginia's coastline, about a hundred miles out. A second ship that I heard about was off of the coast of California," Weston answered.

"Sandra, Duncan, you two seem to know more about this than I do. Where do we go from here? What should we expect? I mean, I've read all the end of the world books. Is it really going to be like *One Second After*?" Blake asked.

"Yes, it really could be that bad. What we ran into yesterday was probably one of the bigger groups we will see. But they were stupid, disorganized. All it would take is someone with a little bit of military training to really put the hurt on us. We really have to look at beefing up our defenses even more," Duncan told them.

"Dad, did you talk to the Cayhills about staying here with us?" Sandra asked.

"Yeah…well…Lisa was so surprised and happy, that's when she—"

"Ha ha, just remember you're not married yet," Sandra told him. Both of the Cayhill boys smiled, and Lisa turned slightly pink in the face, which made them all laugh.

"I'm not speaking for the entire family here, but you guys are further ahead than anyone I've seen out there since we went on the run. If it's okay with you…I mean, we can help. We can work, and we can really contribute. We just don't have anywhere else to go," said Weston, looking sheepish.

"Well," Blake replied, "it's up to you guys. We really could use the extra hands around here. The gardens are coming in, and we just don't have enough hands to put away all the food right now. If any of you guys can help with that…"

"I can help out with that. I spent years canning and putting away food with my mom and grandmother," said Lisa.

"Well, let's see how it goes then. For now, let's show you three where you'll be staying."

The Cayhill family had seen much of the homestead, but Blake went about showing them some of the things they hadn't had the chance to explore yet. He went into more detail about where the traps were, and then showed them the basement and how the homestead still had power. Bobby never quit smiling. The kid thought the whole setup was brilliant, and he had no idea people could really live this way out in the hills. Blake told them about his blog and how that was one of the ways he had made money. He was living the life, writing about it, sometimes publishing the occasional book. Not needing much in the way of material things, he was contented. He explained to them that with his laptop and his air card, he was able to get on the Internet. Until the EMP.

With the scrap lumber in the barn, they figured they had enough to put up a couple of dividers in the basement to give them some privacy. Over the next few days, that's exactly what they did. They went through and rechecked all their traps. Duncan expressed one of his biggest concerns to the group: all of their traps and warning systems were in place on the approach from the lane. If someone were to try to sneak in across the hills out back, they couldn't defend themselves from all angles yet, and they were left wide open.

One other thing that became very apparent rather quickly was the food situation. Their dried goods—things like flour, rice, and spices—were being used at an even faster rate than before. Lisa was a tremendous help in the kitchen, but if they had a couple more canners, the amount of time it would take to preserve foods would be cut in half.

Both sides of the propane burner in Blake's house were always full. The third afternoon the Cayhills were there, Weston shot a young doe out back. Everyone delighted in the deer, and they all debated about whether to smoke it or freeze it. Lisa came to the rescue and suggested they can it. There was no shortage of Ball jars in the barn. She also mentioned that a lot of the canned goods from Blake's grandparents were probably stored in that root cellar.

"I just wish we knew how safe it was out there now. That food truck…" Blake let the words trail off as he considered the possibilities.

"Food truck?" chorused both the Cayhill boys.

CHAPTER 2

Everyone knew that winter was coming, and the rush was on for putting the food away. Blake had told them how bad the roads got around the homestead during the wintertime, and they finally decided that they wanted to risk it. They loaded up Blake's truck and covered trailer, and the men set off down the lane, only to stop and retrieve the two trucks from the raiders.

Sandra was unhappy about being left behind while the men went out to play, as she put it, and Lisa didn't care for it either. Sandra argued that she was the one with the most recent combat experience, and so she should be the one to go. Blake disagreed, pointing out that her skill was the reason why she needed to stay. They needed her to protect the homestead. Blake didn't tell her, but he was

ASHES OF THE WORLD

thinking that of all the people in their group, he was the most expendable.

Lisa knew that putting the food away was really important though. She had pretty much taken over the food storage when she saw how disorganized Blake really was with it, and she teased him about teaching others through his blog. The *Ball Blue Book* was her canning bible, and she had it memorized. It dispelled many of the old wives' tales he'd been taught.

When they finished packing up, Duncan and Blake gave a furious Sandra and Lisa a hug goodbye and drove down the lane towards town. Weston and Bobby drove the trucks from the raiders, and Duncan rode shotgun with Weston, who was in the middle truck. That way, if anything happened, there would be at least one person around who could show them where the food truck was and how to get back to the homestead. Duncan had coached all of the guys on just letting the trucks coast when they could, knowing that even the sound of an idling motor would be loud in this new, still world.

They pulled out of the lane and broke every traffic law in the world as they coasted their way toward the abandoned Walmart truck. Blake pulled out a pair of bolt cutters and a new padlock he had stored in the barn. Duncan watched as Blake cut the lock on the truck and rolled up the door. He put the new lock on the floor by the back of the door and crawled inside.

"You guys...You're never going to believe

this…"

The truck was only about three quarters of the way full. Over half of the truck was filled with food that would last a long time without refrigeration. Blake spotted a pallet jack in the corner. Since it was their main priority, he lined up the camping gear along one side wall as he pulled pallets of food to the end of the truck. Bobby and Weston took turns watching the road in all directions as Blake's vehicle was quickly filled with food. They loaded as much as they possibly could, until the bed of the truck almost rubbed in the wheel wells. The trailer wasn't a whole lot better, but they figured they could get the truck at least to the end of the lane and unload half of it and come back for the rest. Duncan spent most of his time between the day cab and the roof of the semi-trailer, scanning in all directions. He couldn't do much physically with his shoulder still healing. With two, sometimes three of them loading, it didn't take long until all of the pickup trucks were loaded beyond capacity.

"Do you really think just locking it up and leaving it here is safe? Should we maybe post a guard here to make sure no one else gets into it?" asked Bobby.

"No," Duncan said. "We need you and everyone we have to drive. We'll put this lock on that Blake found, and pray to God that no one saw us unloading it and gets the same idea. That's why we drove all three trucks to the trailer at once. A very conspicuous proposition, but we were able to get over half of the food, weren't we?"

"We're a little over halfway. And we didn't grab much of the hunting gear, except for some winter weather stuff for the girls," said Blake, who hopped off the end of the truck and put the new lock in place, pocketing the key.

"How much food is that?" Weston asked Duncan.

"It is not enough for the entire winter, but it's a really good start. If your mom and Blake here keep the food coming in the way it has been, we should be all right. I want to finish unloading the truck as soon as we can. That means at least one more trip."

"Well, let's get moving," said Blake as he made his way to his own rig.

They didn't see anyone the entire trip back to Holloway Lane, so they decided to unhitch the trailer and try to take that up first with both of the Cayhill boys following in the other truck. That meant one truck, one homesteader, and a ton of food left unprotected. Duncan knew his daughter would be furious. That's why he elected to stay behind and guard the trailer. It only delayed the inevitable, but it would give them some time to sit and reflect. Duncan waved goodbye to the other three men and watched as their tail lights slowly disappeared into the darkening gloom of the day.

§ § §

Sandra was the first to hear the motor rolling up the

lane. She warily got her long gun out and set up in position. In this new world of quiet and solitude, sound traveled a long way. One thing she did notice—with the quiet came the sounds of nature that she had missed before. She put her scope on the point of the lane where the first vehicle would enter the property. She smiled in relief when she recognized both trucks, but became concerned when she didn't see the truck her father had been driving.

She could hardly wait until one of the trucks pulled up next to her position and stopped. Her hiding, positioning, and camouflage made it all but impossible for anyone to know she was there. She checked the bed of the trucks to make sure that they hadn't picked up any stray passengers or become unwilling hostages. When she determined everything to be okay, she broke cover and approached Blake's truck. He rolled down the window.

"Blake, where's my dad? What happened with the trailer?" Sandra asked.

"Hey girl, I missed you. Your dad is guarding the trailer. We found so much stuff that we couldn't get all of it. We are overloaded, and there were a couple of spots we worried that we wouldn't even be able to get the trucks up," Blake told her.

"Well, get in and we will rush to the house and get these unloaded as quickly as possible."

Lisa stopped what she was doing in the kitchen long enough to rush out and help them unload as much as she could. When her egg timer went off, she rushed back into the kitchen, then arrived a moment later.

"I took one of the canners off the stove to cool so I can crack the lid. Next one will be due in another twenty minutes. How much more is there?"

Bobby answered for the rest of them, "There's another truck and an overloaded trailer full."

"You know, if you're worried about getting stuck in the lane, it would be smart to send both trucks back down to split the load, and then all three of you can drive back up," Sandra said. She smiled when Blake's jaw dropped open.

"Pure genius!" Blake told her, grinning.

They didn't spend a lot of time getting all of the boxes and bags put up properly. They just started piling it along the walls in the main room of the house. It literally turned into a bucket brigade, except with food. The unloading took about forty minutes. Blake and Weston tried to argue, but Sandra insisted on riding back down with them. The Cayhill boys just shrugged their shoulders and Weston started the truck. They made their way to the lane to let Blake and Sandra have a moment alone.

Blake looked deep into the eyes of the fiery woman. Her gaze was equal parts concern and happiness. She was glad they all made it back safe, and that every ounce of food insured one less day of hunger.

"I was really worried. We need to hurry so we don't leave my dad alone out there with those supplies. Hurry up, or I'll start driving myself."

Both got in, and Blake started driving down the lane a little bit slower than the Cayhill boys, not wanting to catch up with them in a potentially tight spot. Tense minutes passed, but they were all soon reunited. Since Duncan had the bad arm still, Weston and Bobby were already unloading as much of the trailer as they could into the empty truck.

"How's it going?"

"It's been quiet, real quiet," Duncan told them. "Do you think we should unload the entire trailer and just let the trucks handle the weight, or should we split it up between all three?"

"I'd like to not get stuck. That's kind of my plan at this point."

"Some planner you are," Sandra smiled and poked Blake in the ribs.

"Hey! Watch it! I am carrying stuff here."

"Just having a little fun. There's very little of it nowadays."

Duncan smiled. He always trusted his daughter to do the right thing when it came time for marriage. The short time he'd been staying with Blake, he had really come to admire the solitary man who had soon become something of a tribal leader. He knew Blake didn't have any military or combat experience, but what he did have was practical knowledge on how to live and how to survive without anyone else's help or input. He was a thoughtful person, a good listener, and Duncan could see his daughter was falling head over heels in love with him.

ASHES OF THE WORLD

Duncan kept mostly quiet, letting the others do the heavy lifting and occasionally moving some of the smaller bags with his one good arm. He knew the first trip would be the smoothest. It was the next trip to finish unloading the Walmart truck that really bugged him and worried him. Nonetheless, if there was at least that much food left, they really needed to get to it. There were six of them at the homestead now, and that little extra cushion of food would go a long way in easing his fears of a slow starvation in the coming winter months.

The trip back to the homestead went just as smoothly as it had the first time, and they were soon unloading packages once again. They were all drenched in sweat by the time they got unloaded and moved all the trucks behind the barn.

"I can't believe it went that smoothly," Sandra told her father, giving him a hard hug before sitting him down to check on his arm.

"Dad, you tore this open again. You weren't supposed to—"

"I wasn't. It must have been wrestling with that truck."

"It's starting to get red around the edges. Lisa?" she called.

"Yes?"

"Can you take a look at my dad's shoulder? Does this look…"

"Maybe a little. It's going to be red around the edges as it heals."

"Wait, you know what a healing gunshot looks

like?"

"Sure. I worked at a vet's office off and on until I went to college. Stupid hunters would accidentally catch their beagles with bird shots from time to time."

"I'm no dog." Duncan was indignant. "I'm a man of God," he said with a huff, even though the poking and prodding had made him wince more than once.

"You might be," Lisa told him, but she was smiling.

Something in her expression soon had Duncan smiling back, and she laid one hand across his cheek before turning and heading into the house.

"Are we going to get the rest out of the truck tonight?" Bobby asked no one in particular.

"I don't know. I'm pretty bushed, to be honest," Blake said.

"Oh, no you don't," Sandra told him. "You've got canning duty tonight."

"Canning duty is better than unloading trucks. Hey, can I ask you something?" He led her towards the barn for some privacy.

"Sure."

In the shadow of the barn, she took in his expression and knew something was bugging him.

"What is it?" she asked him after he hadn't started to talk.

"When you were in the army…the killing. Did you ever have to…you know?"

"Well, yeah."

"I'm having a hard time sleeping. I keep having

nightmares."

"I think we are all having nightmares, Blake."

"No, I mean, the guys I killed. The quad guys, the ones who shot your dad. The massacre on the hill. It bugs me. It really does."

"That's why I love you."

"Why? Because I can't hardly sleep at night?" His voice was strained, but she knew he was talking about something else.

"No, because it bugs you."

"I don't understand that."

"If you were okay with the killing, well…you wouldn't be you. The fact that it bugs you means that inside here," she poked him in the chest over his heart, "you are a kind and decent man."

"But the Ten Commandments…"

"You worried about 'thou shall not kill'?" she asked him solemnly.

"Yeah, that one."

"In old Hebrew, it literally translates to 'thou shall not commit murder.'"

Blake was silent for a long moment. He looked up at her thoughtfully, and a smile tugged at the corner of his mouth.

"Where does self defense fit in there?"

"You should ask my dad," her eyes sparkled as she leaned in close.

"We're not married yet," Blake whispered as their lips came close to each other.

"We'll have to fix that," she told Blake, leaving him speechless and longing as their kiss deepened.

CHAPTER 3

As they started sorting and stacking all the food, they all felt the effects of the strain and the stress on their bodies. Duncan suggested they wait at least a day or two before heading back out to load up again. He reasoned that if anyone had seen them unloading the trucks, they might come and do the same. If they headed back out there immediately, there was a better than likely chance that they would run into someone, and then a conflict would ensue.

With a hard day's work behind them and empty stomachs, they decided it was time to eat. Everyone helped put a quick meal together with the venison that Weston had shot, along with some potatoes and carrots. There were only four places at the dining room table, so the Cayhill boys stood at the kitchen counter, eating as they all talked.

"Pastor Duncan…" Blake started to say.

"Here it comes. He's getting all official sounding," Duncan said.

"I'm what?"

"You suddenly remember I'm a minister when you're about to ask me something either really important, really personal, or something you really don't want the answer to," he said, speaking with his mouth full.

"Yeah, I want to hear this," Bobby said, grinning. "This is going to be good."

"You two hush," Lisa told the boys.

"Okay then, Duncan, I wanted to talk to you about…well, you see…"

"Daddy, we want you to marry us."

"Well, I'd planned on it."

Duncan's face broke out into a large smile.

"You see…if we're going to wait a couple days before we head back out to the trailer, we were just wondering…"

"You're stammering awful fierce there, Blake. Just spit it out!"

"Daddy, we would like you to marry us before we all head back out to get the rest of food from the truck."

Sandra finished the thought, saving Blake some embarrassment. Putting his thoughts into words for Sandra had eventually gotten easier, once he got used to her. Asking her dad had him tongue-tied. He was very thankful for Sandra stepping in and helping him out.

"Well, in this day and age I imagine there is a little bit of a rush to get things done, isn't there?"

"Every day is a gift at this point. I'd like to make the most of it."

"Amen to that," Duncan smiled at them.

After dinner, Duncan headed back to the trailer. The Cayhill boys went out to the barn to poke through some things and get out of everyone's hair, and Lisa headed down to the basement to the makeshift bed. It was Blake's turn to stay up tonight to get a couple more cycles of canning done. Lisa had filled the canners and left directions scrawled on a scrap of paper laid out under her *Bluebook*.

Raw Packed Beef Stew: 5 pounds of raw beef with all the fat trimmed off. Two pounds of sliced potatoes, two pounds of sliced carrots, a pound of celery, and a pound of onion.

They had been substituting venison for beef, and green beans for the celery, which they didn't have. Garlic, salt, and pepper were also on a per taste basis, according to Lisa's directions.

It was similar to a recipe he'd used in the past, so it was easy to do. Sandra stayed up with him, watching and learning.

"So, we're going to put this in layers."

"How come? Won't it mix while it's cooking?" she asked him.

ASHES OF THE WORLD

"Some," he admitted, "but it's more visual, so we can make sure everything goes in that's supposed to. I think." He was watching her as she worked.

"So we chop all this up and then what?"

"Get the next batch ready. The one pressure canner is almost done with a load, and we'll let it cool enough to take the lid off. And then we'll fill that one up too."

They chopped everything, adding the venison, potatoes, carrots, onions, green beans, garlic, salt, and pepper to each jar in that order, using a wide-mouthed red funnel. Next, they topped it with boiling water.

"Now you have to wipe down the edges with a damp cloth to make sure nothing is on there. You won't get a good seal if you don't."

"Okay, sounds easy. Why are those lids plastic?"

"Oh, those are reusable. See? You put a gasket down first, and then the lid."

"*Tattler.* Ohhh, I remember you writing about these in your blog." She had picked one up to read the label.

"Yeah, pretty cool things. They contacted me a year or two back and offered to let me try them out as long as I'd write about them."

"Wow, they really do that?"

"What? Send out samples for testing? Sure. My blog got five hundred new visitors a day, and half a million visits a month. They were looking for advertising, and I got a lifetime supply of the lids. I didn't make a ton of money off the affiliate links, but…never mind."

His voice had gone sullen and he worked in silence for a few minutes.

"What's wrong?" She hugged him, wrapping her arms around his back, forcing him to stop.

"None of it matters. It's all gone. Nothing is going to be the same."

"No, it isn't. But your blog, I remember the early entries. You said you were learning new skills as well as sharing ones that had been passed down to you. You remember that?"

"Yeah?"

"Well, you probably taught more people how to use a little common sense with the things around them. There's probably people alive today because they read something you wrote about."

"I doubt it," he mumbled, but he didn't sound convinced.

"Besides, if you hadn't written that…we wouldn't have survived. I never would have met you and…"

"Not married yet…" he said suddenly, and she pushed him backwards, laughing.

"Spoil sport."

"Yeah, I know."

"So what do we do now that we have the jars loaded?"

"Put the bands on and use this jar lifter to put them in the canner. The book says eleven pounds of pressure for ninety minutes, and you have to use the chart in here to figure out adjustments because we're in the hills."

She looked over the book.

"Ninety minutes huh? So what do we do in the meantime?" She cocked an eyebrow.

"Well, we uh...I mean…" he stammered under her crooked smile.

"I'm messing with you again. We have another batch to get ready, right?"

"Yeah."

They worked together and set the timer for the pressure canner, unloading the other one when it had cooled and the pressure dropped. They put the contents onto the wooden countertop, and Blake covered them with a towel.

"In case a jar explodes," he explained. It was getting late, and they sat at the table talking, waiting for the last of the batches to be done for the night.

"So, your dad and Lisa?"

"Yeah? What about them?"

"She keeps looking at him."

"You think she likes him?"

"I don't know. I figured you two talk. I mean, you're both girls and—"

"You're close to doing it again."

"Yeah. Well?"

"Well what?"

"What do you think?"

"You know, I never knew my mom. She was always a picture to me, someone my dad always missed. Is that horrible?"

"No, not really," he told her.

"Well, I mean...there have been ladies in the church that have tried to...date? Date my dad? He's never done it, not that I know of."

"Is he lonely?"

"Wouldn't you be? I mean, you lived here alone for a long time."

"I was lonely. I could fix just about anything but that."

"Well, you aren't lonely now, are you?"

"No. I've got more people around me now than I have had in years." He smiled.

"You don't mind it, do you? I mean, us here. Dad, Lisa, Bobby, and Weston?"

"No, actually I don't. I think if it was just me here, I'd go stir crazy, but there comes a point in life where you need someone else. Relying on yourself for everything that grows is tiresome. Now? There's no way I could do this on my own. I'm just thankful I found you." He kissed the top of her head and went and checked on the timer.

"When do you think my dad is going to do the ceremony?"

"Sometime tomorrow. He mentioned something about the boys helping him set up the surprise."

The timer went off, breaking their train of thought, and they headed into the kitchen and pulled the canner off the stove to cool.

"What kind of surprise?" Sandra asked him.

"I don't know; he's your father."

"Your father-in-law after tomorrow." She stuck

her tongue out at him.

"I can't wait to make you mine." He grinned and pulled her close.

"We're not married yet," she chided.

"Soon."

CHAPTER 4

Duncan let everyone but the Cayhill boys sleep in late, leaving the traps to guard the entrance to the homestead. They had everything all staged, and when the old Dodge D fired up and set across the grass up the hill towards the grain silo, the sound of the old diesel woke everybody up. Lisa came padding up the stairs in heavy socks from her bedroom in the basement, and Blake ran to the window, grabbing his long gun to see the truck disappear over the rise behind the barn.

"Sandra, hurry, somebody's got the truck and the trailer," he yelled over his shoulder, waking her up from the recliner in the living room.

"I'm coming." She sprang to her feet, almost falling from being half asleep.

ASHES OF THE WORLD

"Hold on," Bobby said, putting his hand out to stop their progress.

"What's going on?" Lisa asked, moving between them, looking nervously between the guns that Blake and Sandra were now holding and her son's smiling face.

"Somebody's got the truck!"

"No, no. It's part of your surprise. How about you go back to bed?" Bobby said with a grin.

"What surprise? Who's driving it, and why is the trailer hitched to it?"

"Well, you two need someplace to honeymoon, don't you? Duncan and Weston went ahead to set things up. They left me behind to stop you from ruining the surprise. I knew the sound of the motor would wake you up."

"Surprise?" Blake asked again.

"The three of us stripped the trailer and put all clean linens in it and stocked it up for a few days."

"A few days?" Sandra asked. "But we're going into town tomorrow or the day after."

"Well, remember how we stashed the one truck way downhill as a just-in-case?" Bobby looked sheepish.

"Yeah?" Blake asked. A funny feeling was beginning to develop in his stomach.

"Well, I uh...I'm actually staying behind because I took one truck and the enclosed trailer. Weston and I both did, that is. Your dad was pissed, but I guess I'd rather have a minister mad at me than my mom."

"Where is everything?" Blake asked, incredulous.

"Still in the two trucks and trailer. I've got it hidden deep in the brush."

"You've been up all night? Why would you risk all of that?" Lisa interjected, sounding half awed and half pissed.

"Killing them with kindness," Bobby shot back, but he looked nervous.

"Why?"

"Mom, if they hadn't taken us in and stopped those guys…We owe them a lot. Once we convinced Pastor Duncan not to shoot us for going off alone, we just wanted to let Ms. Sandra and Blake here have a real honeymoon type of thing. We just didn't have any place fancy to send them, so Duncan mentioned the camper trailer, and that's how we…"

"Of all the harebrained, foolhardy, dangerous…"

Lisa continued going off on them, and Blake stepped back inside with Sandra on his arm. They headed into the basement. Sandra's stomach growled when he pulled a side cut of bacon out and some onions and cheese he had in the converted fridge.

"Omelets?"

"No eggs. We have to find some chickens if we want some eggs."

"Ahhh, so the bacon, hash-brown dish thing."

"Are you getting sick of it?"

ASHES OF THE WORLD

"No, because I'm with you. I want some eggs, but this bacon is some of the best ever…"

"We can go out back and shoot a hog just about every day if you really love it that much."

"Then why are we killing ourselves growing this huge garden?"

"Because, you need variety in your diet to help support—"

"I'm kidding." She poked him in the ribs and took off at a dead run up the stairs, where a red-faced Blake finally caught up with her. Upstairs, they caught the tail end of Lisa's tirade.

"…And you do something stupid like this? I thought I raised you two better."

"Sorry, Mom," both boys chorused.

Blake and Sandra cooked up a big skillet of food, the cast iron pan keeping things warm long after it was removed from heat. After breakfast, Lisa headed outside with Bobby to finish ruining his morning by lecturing him about the unexpected trip. Blake and Sandra were quiet and avoided eye contact. Not because they were nervous about today, but because of what it meant. Sandra was trying to swallow the enormity of what Bobby and Weston had done, the risks they had taken. She'd been out on enough patrols to know that their timing was probably perfect in that it was immediately after they hit the truck yesterday, and they had gone sometime after dark.

If anyone had been scoping the food truck out, looking to finish the job, they were probably scared off by the vehicle from earlier coming back. She had wondered how they were able to get the rest of the semi unloaded with just one truck and trailer, but remembered they said something about the second truck being full as well. She reckoned that they had to unload part of the supplies into the second one and make two trips. That was risky.

"You know, I figure those boys had to have made two trips to get all that stuff." Sandra voiced her thoughts.

"Yeah, I was considering that as well."

"Why do you think they did it? I mean, that was a pretty big gesture."

"You know what those raiders had in store for their mom, don't you?" he asked softly.

"Well…"

"Rape, enslavement, torture, murder."

"You can't possibly know that." Sandra's horrified expression betrayed the fact that she had thought that as well.

"They all but said that. The three raiders that come up here had that in mind when they saw you too."

"Okay, you're probably right. I just can't figure out the why."

"I think Bobby was being literal. If we hadn't taken them in, they would have had to live off the land or become raiders themselves."

"That's depressing."

"Yeah. It's hard to argue with an empty stomach. People do all sorts of things when they are desperate and sick with fear," Blake said, scooping some food onto two plates.

"I know, I've seen it when I was...over there." She just nodded outside, but Blake knew what she meant.

The front door flew open, and a red-faced Lisa stormed in with a shame-faced Bobby following her. He gave them a halfhearted smile and headed over to the food.

"Your mom chew your ears off?"

"And half of my backside," he said, but he was still grinning.

"Don't think I'm done with you two. When your brother gets back—" Lisa stopped ranting when she saw the three of them looking at her. "Well, what they did was foolish," she tried to explain.

"If I promise we won't do something like that again, would that help?"

"No. At least not yet. Your brother isn't back yet, and trust me, I plan on having words with him too."

Blake and Sandra took their plates and headed out the front door to sit on the porch. Bobby gave them a pleading look, but Blake just shrugged his shoulders and closed the front door behind them to let the abuse continue.

"I hope Lisa doesn't remember the backpack with the grenades," Sandra said, trying not to laugh.

"I know. I think she plans on skinning her boys alive."

Sandra slid close to him, until she was snuggled into Blake's side. They ate in relative peace, but were occasionally disrupted by the sound of raised voices behind them. They both thought they understood Lisa's reasoning, and had a basic grasp of what the boys did. It was very impressive. The Cayhills were a tight-knit family, one that was willing to help and fight for each other. Blake finished his food first and enjoyed the warmth of Sandra's closeness. She finished soon enough, and he took both plates and set them aside. He pulled her close, kissing the side of her temple.

"You know, for the first time in my life, I don't feel so lonely. I'm actually pretty happy considering everything that's gone on."

"Me too. In just a little while we're going to be married and..." She gave him an exaggerated wink.

"Preacher's daughter," he chuckled. She gave him a playful push, almost knocking him off the top step they were sitting on.

He let out a mock growl, and she yelled and took off running. For a minute, the two of them ran through the tall grass that surrounded the barn until Blake finally caught up with her. He grabbed her, and they both tumbled playfully to the ground like they were teenagers. They wrestled around for a moment, their breathing becoming heavy. The air felt charged around them. Sandra broke off, and Blake noticed her shift in attitude immediately.

"What is it, hon?"

"That little dip with the double doors. I never noticed that before."

"Oh that. It's the old staircase to the root cellar."

ASHES OF THE WORLD

"I never saw another set of doors down there."

"My grandparents said it was blocked off when they were kids. I checked them out when I got the property. Just opens to an old block wall."

"None of the root cellar has any brickwork, just mortared fieldstone."

"Hm. I don't know. We'll check it out sometime."

Blake was trying not to spoil the moment and loved how close together their bodies were. He was about to make another suggestion, but the rumble of the Dodge D filled the air. They both scrambled up, brushing each other off before jogging back to the front porch. Lisa was still scolding Bobby by the sound of it, and they sat on the porch, trying to look innocent as Duncan and Weston pulled to a stop.

"Since you're both sitting there, I'm going to assume you figured things out?" Duncan asked, stepping out, with Weston following suit a moment later.

"Bobby spilled the beans. Lisa's not too happy about the boys though," Sandra told them, trying to keep a straight face.

"Yeah, you may want to duck when you walk in there, Weston," Blake told him and almost laughed at the pained expression on his face.

"You didn't tell your mother?" Duncan rounded on him.

"No, she wouldn't have approved."

"Thank you, both of you," Sandra told him, trying to change the subject.

"Just a small part of what we owe you guys. What time is the party? I want to try to get a nap in now the heavy lifting is all done."

"How about nightfall?"

"Okay then. I have plenty of time."

Weston gave them one long look before opening the front door. Lisa's voice immediately changed volume, and he closed the door, cutting off the worst of the chewing out from everyone else's hearing.

"Think we should give them a minute?" Duncan asked.

"I would." Blake picked up their forgotten plates and put them on the railing so he wouldn't forget them when it was safe to go inside.

"Hey Daddy, we found something of a mystery. Want to check it out so we can let Lisa vent?"

CHAPTER 5

Duncan was unimpressed with the walled-off section once they got the doors open. The mortaring on the blocks was old, older than he was. He promised to look things over in a day or two and make sure the food storage was going to be safe from outside entrances. That was his biggest fear—using the cellar as a last resort refuge only to have somebody push their way in from the outside. That morning, they had left the approach to the lane unattended.

They were all ready to head back to the house and make sure everything was okay. And that Lisa hadn't killed off her sons.

When Duncan, Blake and Sandra got back to the house, both boys were smiling, but in a guilty-looking way. Lisa's angry gaze was still fixed on her boys.

"You know, this is supposed to be a day of celebration." Duncan gestured to her.

Lisa's face transformed when she caught sight of Duncan. She'd meant to give him a little bit of the snark she'd shared with her boys, but something about the man had been getting to her, and it was all she could do not to repeat the hasty kiss she had shared with him. Her husband had been gone for a long while, and there'd never been another love. Something about the big burly preacher tugged at her heartstrings. She'd held back, but she could tell by the way he gave her a kind smile, or his hand would brush hers, that he shyly had returned at least some sense of fondness. She shook her head to clear it.

"It is. I just wish you three would have let me in on the scheme."

"Wouldn't have been much of a surprise if we did that, Mom." Bobby told her, turning to put an arm around her as she stood on the front porch. "You would have screamed at us not to go, and it would have woken up everybody."

"I wouldn't have…"

"You would have, Mom. Really, we're not your little boys anymore. We've grown. I've been in the police department for a few years now, and Bobby was ready to head off to West Point this fall," Weston told her, a sardonic smile stretched across his features. "Besides—"

"You're always going to be your mother's babies." Duncan's booming voice closed the subject. "Now Lisa, how about the surprise that we set up for the kids?"

"Your surprise?" Sandra asked her dad, turning to poke him in the ribs.

"Yeah, what're you talking about?" Blake gave him a puzzled grin.

"Well, your bride has to have a beautiful dress."

"But we don't have anything like that…" Sandra's voice trailed away as Lisa smiled big and dragged her into the house, shutting the main bedroom door.

"Uh, Duncan?"

"Just go with it, kid. Come on Cayhills, let's set up the picnic. We'll cook food as we go later. This is going to be a country-style wedding, and I'm going to need you all to get scarce so Lisa and I can work on getting everything all set."

Duncan headed inside. Blake just looked at the Cayhill boys and then shook his head. He headed out to the barn, the brothers trailing close behind. Blake wondered if they'd help set everything up. It was apparent that they spent all of their time physically moving things instead of moving the trucks up to the compound. Blake filled Bobby and Weston in on the idea he had, and they readily agreed so they set to work.

"You know, this is supposed to be her wedding day. And you're lining up all kinds of work," Bobby complained, only halfheartedly.

"Yeah, yeah I know. We have to get the rest of

the food up here. I never went through the rest of the truck; did you see anything that looked interesting?"

"Yeah, we snagged some of that camping gear, and some of the things from the hardware section."

"Was there anything good?"

"The hardware pallet had stuff that looked like it would be interesting; I got enough wire and miscellaneous fittings to make a set of snares," Bobby said excitedly.

"You two know how to make snares?" Blake asked them.

"Well, no," Bobby said.

"We were figuring you did," Weston finished.

"I do. Let's get the truck and trailer up here. Then I'll show you two how to build them. It's pretty easy stuff."

"Don't you have to get ready?"

"Honestly, I have time, and if I don't stay busy…" Blake's voice trailed off as he looked at the house.

"You'll run from the altar?"

"With her dad as the preacher to boot? I'd be double damned."

They all laughed at that, and Blake grabbed his long gun from the house and walked down the lane towards the stashed truck. It would take them awhile, but Blake felt a nervous excitement and had extra energy to burn. It was like a pressure had built in his chest, and it was both a wonderful and scary feeling at the same time. If he stopped to think how much his life was about to change again, he was

ASHES OF THE WORLD

worried he'd die of fright. The Cayhill men kept up a constant muted chatter, walking ten to fifteen apart, picking their way slowly and using the trees for cover.

In this silent new world, every sound was magnified, and they whispered back and forth, marveling at how far the sound traveled. They took the opportunity to move quietly, and they moved off the lane so Blake could show them how he traveled silently in the woods. He advised them to always look at the layout and plan a pathway. "Choose a path, if possible, where you aren't stepping on dry, brittle leaves or stepping on brush. With the mental plan in place, you move slowly at first, heel to toe, feeling the ground under you. Use natural game trails, and avoid branches that brush against you." He taught them every other trick he could think of to keep quiet and not leave a scent around.

These were basic things he learned from a lifetime of hunting and the school of hard knocks. Once they were shown this way of walking, they practiced awkwardly, and although it took them awhile, they made it to the trucks with only scaring up one deer, which ran off and snorted at them, stamping one foot on the ground.

"Probably caught our scent. If he would have seen us, he wouldn't have stomped."

"Why didn't we shoot it?" Bobby asked, keeping his voice just as quiet as Blake's whisper.

"I don't want to process today. I got plans for later on," he winked.

BOYD CRAVEN

The route back up to the homestead required somebody to walk in front of the truck, to disarm and reset the traps. One guy could do it, but with three of them, it went quite a bit faster. Blake noticed gaps in the traps that he wanted to address later. He also made a note to drag brush in front of the trees that were pockmarked by buckshot from when the gang had come after Lisa. Bobby reset the traps, and Weston was driving the second pickup.

Everyone breathed easier once they got past the shotgun rat traps. Those things were just as dangerous to them as they were to somebody tripping them. When they were finally through, they started to unload everything onto the front porch. Neither of the Cayhill boys dared enter the house, and Blake wasn't in a hurry now either. They stacked cases of food, camping and fishing gear, and some of the hardware items nearby. Blake held back and smiled at some of the materials for snare building. He motioned for Bobby and Weston to follow him.

"Looks like we still have some time to burn," Bobby said, wiping sweat off his face.

"Yeah, let me give you the rundown on building some snares. Maybe you can try some out. First thing you have to do is cut some of this cable into usable lengths."

"How do you know what size to use?" Weston asked.

"Well, for rabbits and squirrels, you only want a small hoop for their head. Maybe this big." He held his hands together, forming a circle about four inches wide. "Then you want at least ten inches of cable before you have whatever you're tying it off of. That way, your wire goes farther. Or for hogs, maybe a hoop about a foot or so, leaving the cable about six inches long to tie onto something sturdy. "

"Wait, if you can snare hogs, can you snare deer?" Bobby was all smiles.

"Well, it's illegal to snare deer…" A dawning realization lit up his face. "Wait…I guess that doesn't apply anymore. If smell carries forever, I'm sure the sound of us hunting meat would as well."

"Oh yeah. I'm sure it would. But folks would be foolish to come up this way after you guys took out those invaders. It probably sounded like World War Three going on."

"How do the critters not pull out of the snare?" Weston asked, having made a loop with his hands and observing how the wire slid easily.

"Well, we don't have Camlocks. We'll have to improvise."

"Camlocks?"

"It's a brand name of snare fitting. It pulls tight, won't let go, and strangles the animal. Never could legally use them on the bigger critters, but now…"

"It doesn't matter."

"Nope."

They went through the hardware pile and found some galvanized L-shaped brackets with a single screw hole in them about three quarters of an inch wide. Then he dug through the fishing supplies and pulled out several packages of lead sinkers in a tear drop shape. He slid the sinker on a piece of 5/16-inch cable and slid the cable through the bracket's hole. He then made a small loop and pulled the sinker down the line until he slid the end of the cable through it. He pulled out as much slack as he could, leaving a little bit of the cable end hanging out, then put the sinker on the edge of the work bench and hit it several times, flattening the lead. He ran the free end of the cable through the remaining eye hole of the bracket and slid a second sinker on it. He made another small loop on the end and hammered the second sinker flat as well.

"It's the wrong time of the year for walnuts, but you soak the green husks in water and make a dye out of them. It gives the snares a camo look. The small loop here is where you tie off the snare to a tree, log or whatever. You can build smaller snares for rabbits and squirrels, but those are usually spring loaded and you won't need something to make it lock."

Weston took the completed snare and put his arm through the loop and pulled it tight, feeling the wire hold firm. "Do you think a hog could break this?"

"Or what about a deer?" Bobby asked.

"Well, I think the cable will hold. The sinkers and the bracket are the weakest points, but you don't have to hold the animals forever. They'll weaken fast when their air is cut off. I've never snared a hog before…"

"But have you snared deer?" The former Green-

ASHES OF THE WORLD

ville police officer asked him, smiling as Blake squirmed.

"I'll plead the fifth, officer."

They all chuckled at that and made a variety of snares as the hours passed. Bobby figured out how to put a bend in the line so the snare would stay open at the right length of the loop they wanted to make. They then rolled everything back up and talked about setting and baiting them along the pathways when they were interrupted by Duncan.

"Blake, it's time."

CHAPTER 6

The one piece of advice that Blake remembered was to not lock his knees as they stood during the ceremony. Duncan recited the service by memory, and the Cayhill clan stood as friends and witnesses. They didn't have rings to share, but under God's law, two became one. Sandra nervously initiated the kiss when the final words were spoken, and when the kiss deepened, Duncan grunted and then cleared his throat several times before Blake pulled back, his eyes dazed.

"You two, uh…Your honeymoon hasn't started yet…" Duncan sputtered. "Ladies and gentlemen, I'd like to introduce you to Mr. and Mrs. Blake Jackson."

"Your last name is Jackson?" Sandra asked him

in almost a whisper.

"Yeah, where do you think the J from Back Country J came from?" He tried to talk out of the side of his mouth, but everyone heard, and they were all smiling.

"It's your last name now too, Sandra."

"Daddy." Sandra's smile was radiant.

They feasted on smoked ham and baked potatoes seasoned with wild onion that Lisa had found. Bottles of fruit wine were passed around, and soon the two newlyweds took a pair of quads from the barn and drove to the top of the rise where the camper was parked.

"You know, I have to find me a girlfriend," Bobby said, watching the quads disappear in the distance.

"You have to find a life first," Weston joked.

"Want to go set some of those snares?"

"Yeah, let's hurry before Mom—"

"No you don't," Lisa interjected. "Blake and Ms. Sandra may be on a short vacation, but we still have a ton of food to put up. You can go play tomorrow." Her voice was kind, but firm.

"Yes ma'am," they chorused.

Duncan smiled at the adult boys listening to their mother. The brothers were full of respect with regards to how they spoke and acted around her. He hadn't seen that often, and he remembered all the kind smiles she'd dropped in his direction, even the kiss she'd given him the night they'd asked her family to move in. He mentally went through the list of tasks they still had to accomplish. His healing gunshot wound had almost run them out of medical supplies entirely. They were almost ready to start boiling clean sheets and foraging for herbs, but he knew with the winter coming, they would have to make some more trips off the homestead.

Much like his daughter, Pastor Duncan loved lists. He knew that "the homestead," as they had all started calling it, was almost perfect for weathering out the storm of fear and violence that would be sweeping the rest of the country. He had been the only man in his daughter's life till now, and today would be the happiest and saddest day he could remember. So he sat on the front step of the house, pulled out a notebook, and started jotting things down.

Food – Any and all. Never have enough for now.

Clothing – Boots, all weather gear. Blake doesn't have clothing for everyone, but Lisa and Sandra would be fine for a while.

Bleach – Sterilizing and making suspect water clean and safe. Just in case.

Medical Supplies – Any and all.

Ammunition – Ammo or reloading supplies. Remember to ask Blake if he has that kind of stuff.

Guns – We have plenty, but common caliber would make life easier.

Livestock – Chickens! Maybe a cow, rabbits? Ducks?

Survivors – We need more help here. Our traps saved us the first time. We won't be able to do that every time.

He was startled when somebody sat down next to him and scooted in close. Lisa pulled herself tight against him and gave him a one-armed hug.

"You know, you never get to keep them," she said, referring to Sandra.

"I know. It's been just her and me for so long now. I'll get over it."

"What are you writing there?"

"Just listing some things for the next time we leave the homestead."

"Let me see."

She read in silence for a while and nodded. She handed him back the list and just sat there, looking off into the night.

"Do you think it's ever going to get better, Pastor?"

"Call me Duncan. And yes, I think it will. Not just yet though."

"How can you be so sure?"

"Faith," he said, fingering the cross on his necklace. He put a beefy arm around her shoulders and pulled her in. "Just faith."

§ § §

Bobby and Weston awoke just as they heard Duncan closing the front door. He'd stayed in the little bedroom the previous night and had already changed out the linens. By the look of his camo, he was heading out to do his lookout duties. They both kept quiet as they dressed quickly and eased out to the barn without disturbing their mother. She'd stayed up late talking to the big man, and neither of them had seen her take a shining to anyone since their dad had died.

"So, in a zombie apocalypse, who would marry off the minister if he's the one getting hitched?" Bobby asked.

"I don't know, another minister? This isn't a zombie apocalypse though. It's probably a full-scale nuclear war now."

"Yeah, I know. That scares me. That's why zombies sound more fun."

"There's nothing fun about what's happening in the world right now," Weston told him.

"I know, but it takes my mind off things."

"How about we focus on those snares and finding a good game trail or path to set them up on? That pork is running out fast."

"You want to get another pig?"

"If we can. But any meat at this point sounds good."

"I hear you."

With no specific chores to do that day, they both decided to concentrate on some hunting or trapping. Weston had brought a small .22 rifle with some subsonic short rounds for small game. He

ASHES OF THE WORLD

didn't want to use a larger gun, knowing the whip/ crack sound of a heavier load would travel forever, but a subsonic round wouldn't go as far.

They headed to the northeastern portion of the property, close to where Blake had killed the hog, and searched the tree line at the edge of the old hay field. They found tunnels through the dark grass leading to the tree line, so they set some of the small game snares they made and used a spool of bank line to secure them. They hadn't figured out how to do the spring-style traps yet, but Blake assured them that almost all animals are used to pushing through grass and branches to some extent, and feeling the brush of the wire wouldn't disturb them until it was tight around their neck, and far too late.

They moved on, sipping water out of their bottles when they got too hot. They found some larger game trails that Weston assured his younger brother were made by deer. He hung a snare almost thirty inches off the ground, and farther on he hung another two sets, both higher and lower than the first. Since they weren't able to ask Blake, they wanted to cover all of their bases. They were heading back when they heard the crack of a rifle. Both took off at a dead run toward the house.

"Damn it," Weston swore. "I didn't bring a pistol. All I've got is this squirrel gun."

"I've got my .45," Bobby panted, keeping pace with his brother's long-legged stride.

They paused at the house long enough for Weston to grab his guns, and he raced back out to catch up with Bobby, who was already getting into the ambush position that Weston and Blake had used on the convicts. Weston took up a position near the toe tappers and started scoping the area.

"See anything?" Bobby hissed, almost silent as the wind.

"Yeah, Duncan's got some folks at gunpoint."

"Do you think we should..."

"Stay put," Weston whispered, watching the two figures stand frozen by the bore of Duncan's gun.

Duncan slowly approached the two figures. He pulled a ball cap off one, letting blonde hair spill free. A girl, maybe a teenager. The brothers got a good look at the second figure and saw that it was a teenage boy. He looked so much like the girl that the two could be twins. Duncan had the boy lift his shirt, and he patted the back of his pants. The good preacher raised one hand and waved in the distance. There was no way he knew for certain someone was behind him, but he was counting on everyone to react to his signal the way they had discussed at the dinner table a time or two.

The Cayhill brothers broke cover and walked slowly with their guns at the ready. It took them some minutes, but soon enough they came to Holloway Lane to meet the pastor and the two kids being held at gunpoint.

"Afternoon, Pastor. Have the hogs been fed yet?" Bobby said, breaking the silence.

The strangers hadn't heard their approach, so when Bobby's question floated out of the darkening day, they jumped.

"Jesus, mister," the startled girl exclaimed.

"Who are you?" Weston asked.

"Melissa. And that's my brother, James. We're looking for a place to stay."

"I'm sorry, kids, this is private property." Duncan's tone was harsh, and not at all the jovial, happy-go-lucky pastor that they had gotten used to hearing.

"Please, mister?" James begged. "We've got no place to go, and we're awful hungry."

"Move on, kids. Go straight back down this trail. Turn east or west at the road. I don't care which way."

"How about some food? Do you have any food to share?" Melissa asked, no longer looking fearful. She stepped closer to Duncan, making him raise the gun higher.

"No, I don't have anything—"

"Here." Bobby held out a Ziploc bag of smoked ham slices. "It's kind of like jerky. Take it and do what the preacher says."

Duncan's gaze shot daggers at Bobby, but he didn't say anything. Melissa reached up and took the bag, and Bobby fell back, getting his distance again, his .45 held loosely at his side.

"Now go on," Weston said, his rifle now raised, but pointing between the two kids.

"Wait, kids," Duncan said, his tone sharp. "Don't come back here. We've got lethal traps all over. Forget about this place."

"You don't own all of this," the boy said angrily, pointing to the woods and the fields.

"We actually do. Now I suggest you move, and if you stray off the lane here, you may set off something that will have dire consequences. Now get out of here!" The last was shouted, and the look of fear returned to their features. They turned and walked away slowly, mumbling.

The three men watched them in silence until they couldn't see them anymore.

"Duncan, what the holy hell was that about?" Weston finally spoke, bewildered. Bobby looked upset with the preacher.

"Something about them wasn't right."

"What do you mean?"

"They were too clean, too well fed. Hell, the girl was wearing perfume."

"So they were acting normal, and you run them out at gunpoint?" Bobby's tone was tight, but you could hear the anger in it.

"Cut your tone, Bobby. Something about them was off. They weren't running scared, and they should have been. They were spotless, and the world from the highway is all ashes as far as I could see. They were asking for food, but they didn't look hungry or thirsty."

"So they have to be sick and starving for you to—"

"Shut up, Bobby," Weston said softly, cutting his brother off. "Duncan probably had good reason."

"But I thought you wanted to find survivors. I

thought we needed more help?"

"We do, but we're not just bringing anybody in."

"Just drop it for now, Bobby," Weston said.

Bobby stomped off, all pretense of stealth gone. In the gloom, they lost sight of him after a few minutes.

"I'm sorry, I wish I could explain better what I felt and why I didn't think those kids—"

"Duncan, one thing I learned in the police department that I hold near and dear. Follow your instincts. You'll live longer."

"You're brother going to stay pissed at me forever?"

"I doubt it. Probably reacted the way he did because he's young, and Melissa caught his eye."

"She did? But she's just a kid."

"He's barely 20. She can't be too much younger."

"Well I'll be. Maybe you're right. It just felt like a trap to me."

"Yeah, something felt off," Weston agreed.

"We going to wait here for a while and make sure they don't come back?"

"I am. Probably for a few more hours."

"It's getting dark out. How about we wait an hour or so, then we head back in."

"You don't have to wait with me."

"I know, but if I come home without you, my mother'll skin me alive."

"Yeah, she's feisty, that one."

"You have no idea. Yet."

"Yet?"

"Yeah, she's taken a shine to you, preacher."

Duncan just shook his head and fell silent, a faint smile touching his features. Weston took up his position southwest of Duncan, but kept him in sight and hunkered down to wait.

CHAPTER 7

L isa listened from her makeshift bedroom in the basement as the men argued above her. She pretended to be asleep, but she was wrestling with her thoughts and feelings. Since the world had blown up, she'd been an emotional wreck, and she knew she was taking it out on her sons. Now it sounded like Bobby was upset with Duncan, and she didn't know what to do. They spoke in angry tones at the dining room table, but no words were decipherable to her. She desperately wanted to find out what was going on, but she didn't want to make things worse.

Her sons explained over and over why they went to unload that truck in the dead of night, but none of it mattered when compared to what could have happened. She was blown away by the kindness, bravery, and generosity of Duncan and the Jacksons. They had immediately made a place for her and her boys, and she didn't feel like they were doing enough in return. Now they were fighting above her.

"… But you can't know…"

"They could have…"

"Why don't…Who cares?"

"…Blake and Sandra."

Words started coming to her the longer she listened, and she jumped when one of the freezers in the next room started. The quiet compressor was the loudest noise down there, and it drowned out any clear sounds of the argument above. After a while, she heard the door close, and her boys headed down to the basement.

"Is everything okay?" she asked, sitting up.

"Yeah, just a disagreement," Bobby said, smiling.

"It sounded like you were arguing with Duncan."

"He kind of was, but he understands now," Weston answered for him.

"So everyone is good?"

"Yes, Mom. I'm bushed."

The boys headed to their own partitioned off room and bunked down. Soon she heard their soft snores. Sleep didn't come easy, and she could hear the bed upstairs creaking as Duncan tossed and turned. She was wondering if the uneasiness she felt was also reflected in his heart. More and more every day, she grew fonder of the burly man. So much so it almost hurt. When sleep did find her finally, she dreamed of the wedding, but not Blake and Sandra's. She smiled as she slept.

§ § §

"You boys slow down," Lisa hollered as Bobby and Weston were headed out the door. "I've got a ton of canning to do today, and I need you to bring me four cases of jars from the root cellar."

"How fast do you need them?" Weston asked.

"In an hour."

"Good. We can go check the traps out and bring those on our way back through," Bobby said, almost bouncing with energy.

"Traps?" Lisa was bewildered.

"Yeah. Blake showed us how to make some snares. We're running low on pork, and it wouldn't hurt to learn a new way to hunt that doesn't make a lot of sound."

"Are they safe?"

"Very safe. We're taking guns as a backup," Weston told her.

"Okay, well, bring me those jars as soon as you can."

"You got it, Mom."

Bobby's enthusiasm was infectious, and gone was the angry, sullen boy from yesterday. Weston could hardly keep up with his fast stride and broke into a jog a couple of times until they made it to the first set of traps. The first few sets were empty, but the last one in the string had a fat rabbit in it. They walked to the larger snares with a smile, using their scopes on their rifles to check out the land ahead of them. They could see something lying down in the grass near the first set. The boys stopped, waiting almost two hundred yards away, watching.

When they saw no movement, they crept up to the snare set. A fat doe had walked through the set and expired almost underneath the tree the line was tied to. Weston pulled out his hunting knife to begin skinning it, but Bobby stopped him.

"Let's go check the other two first." He was visibly excited. He felt that this meat had practically given itself to them because of the knowledge and skill between his older brother and Blake's ingenuity, and he wanted to see if they had anything else.

"You go ahead. I'm going to gut this one first. If you don't get to it quick, it can spoil the meat. Come let me know if you get any more. I'll gut it for you."

"You know, it won't make me puke forever."

"It probably will this time. That's why you're heading off alone."

"Shut up, Weston," he said lightly, teasing him right back. But his brother was right. It wasn't something he'd ever been able to do without throwing up the few times he tried.

"Fire a shot if there's any issues, and I'll come find you."

With happy thoughts, Bobby headed to the next set. It was empty, and he could hear something breaking branches probably a hundred yards deeper into the woods. He approached slowly to witness the last moments of a younger deer kicking the air as it too died. Bobby was slightly shaken by the scene of death, but he knew the meat would be greatly needed. He loved venison, and had tried to be the hunter that his older brother was and that his father had been, but he hadn't quite gotten over the death, blood, and guts part of it. Once that was done, he was fine. He could and had done it, but it still made him uneasy.

Bobby looked around and found a fairly straight branch the diameter of his finger. He used his belt knife to cut it off. From six feet away, he slowly tapped the deer's eyeball with the branch, ready to bolt if it was playing opossum. He'd listened to his father and brother always coach him to do this, to make sure it truly wasn't alive. Nothing alive can stand having its eyeball touched. The reason for this was twofold. First, a deer will lie down and not move, trusting its camouflage and stillness to keep it from predators. Not all the time, but quite a bit. Second point, deer have sharp hooves and can break bones and kick a hole in your stomach if you aren't careful. So the eye poke was important.

Bobby dropped the branch and sheathed his knife. He worked the snare loose by using both hands, sliding the loop up and off, letting the limp head and neck drop to the earth.

"This one's small enough that I can probably carry it back," he muttered to himself.

"Can we have it?" The feminine voice startled him, and he fell onto his back.

Looking up, James and Melissa were half standing behind a tree, twenty feet away.

"What are you doing here?" He pulled his rifle off his shoulder, remembering the disagreement the night before.

"We're looking for food. And a place to stay."

"I mean, how did you get up here?"

"Oh, well, when we found your first set of traps, we headed into the forest. We've been walking in what feels like a big circle," James answered.

"Yeah, one big circle."

"You two don't look like you spent the night in the woods. Hold it right there." He pointed the rifle between them when they started approaching him.

They stopped moving immediately, and James stepped in front of his sister.

"We're just hungry," he told Bobby.

"You know how to gut one of these things?" he asked, looking at the deer and then to them, the point on his rifle waving back and forth.

"No, but we can learn. We really need the food. Could you show us?" Melissa asked.

It was something in her tone of voice, or the way the sunlight hit her hair, but Bobby's resolve melted, and he lowered the rifle and leaned it up against the tree the snare was tied off to. He pulled his belt knife out and took a deep breath.

"Come watch then. I'm Bobby, by the way," he told them. He considered offering his hand out to shake, but saw the look on James's face and thought better of it.

"Is there anyone else out here with you? I mean, I don't want to get you in trouble with that big grouch," Melissa said.

"No," he lied. "But they will come looking for me if we don't do this quick."

He cut the deer's throat and pulled it on its back, spreading its legs open.

"The trick is to cut here. Not too deep. You just want to open the cavity and not puncture the guts. That'll spoil the—"

The heavy branch that hit him came from behind. His right ear blossomed in pain, and he felt himself falling, landing beside the deer. His vision grew hazy as he fought for consciousness. He was helpless as he felt his pockets emptied and his .45 removed from his holster. Someone was working on his boots when he heard a shout and a gunshot.

§ § §

"Hey bro, it's okay. I got you. Wake up man, its okay." Weston's voice brought sharp focus to the world again.

When Bobby sat up, Weston felt a surge of relief. He'd known his brother wouldn't have gutted a deer on his own, but if he had, he could have done the job two or three times already, so he went to investigate. He had come across James rifling through his brother's pockets. He'd fired a snap shot at James, and only succeeded in making him fall flat on his rear. The kid used the dense woods for cover as he made his escape. Weston had thought about chasing him, but he was more worried about the bloody mess of his brother's face.

"What happened?" Bobby rolled onto his knees and started dry heaving.

"Easy man. You got hit on the head. Probably have a concussion."

"The girl said—"

"What girl? I saw James. Was that blonde here too?"

"Melissa. They wanted to see how to gut a—" His dry heaves turned into wet ones, and soon the sounds of the woods were full of that noise.

"Shit." Weston pulled off his pack and got out a bottle of water and a handkerchief. He wetted it down and then poured water across the back of Bobby's head, washing away the dirt and dead leaves that covered the injured side of his face. Other than some superficial scratches, his right ear looked shredded where something sharp on the branch had scraped the fragile flesh raw, making it bleed profusely.

"They got the deer," he said, sitting up and moving himself away from the mess.

"Who got the deer?"

"James and Melissa."

"You had one here?"

"Yeah, probably the fawn of the one you were gutting."

ASHES OF THE WORLD

"Was it in spots?"

"No. It just—" He let out a wet burp, and it almost sounded like he was going to start vomiting again. When his stomach finally settled, Weston handed him the wet washcloth.

"For your…" Weston motioned his hand in a circle around his face.

Bobby tried to nod, but the motion made him queasy all over again. He used the wet cloth to wipe the sweat and dirt from the main part of his face, careful not to touch his ear. He grimaced when Weston pulled out a pair of socks from his pack.

"I hope those are clean."

"Clean enough," he joked.

"Why do you carry extra socks?" He knew he was wasting time, but he didn't feel sturdy enough yet to stand on his own.

"Blisters. All right, get up and let's see."

Bobby took his brother's offered hand and was half pulled to his feet. He held on to a nearby sapling for support and held still until his brother touched his ear with the sock to staunch the flow of blood. The pain shot through the dizziness, but it didn't help the queasy feeling in his stomach. Weston watched his brother battle to keep the rest of his breakfast down and then finally steady himself.

"You okay?" Weston asked him, letting his brother hold pressure on the ear now.

"I think so. I need to change," he looked down at his shirt.

"Don't worry about that. Let's get you safe, then

we'll go after them."

"For what? Being hungry?"

"They stole your stuff, and they could have killed you, bro." Bobby was slumping sideways now, and Weston had to move quickly to catch him before he hit the ground. "Shit."

§ § §

Duncan heard the first shot, and when none repeated, he went back to studying the foliage around the lane. The Cayhill boys had been talking about some fresh meat, finding something to throw on the smoker, so he figured they had gotten lucky. The twins from yesterday had him shook up, and he didn't quite know what it was about them, so instead of staying stationary, he started patrolling the area around the lane in a semi circle, making it wider and wider. He was unsettled by how close they got and how unafraid they seemed to be. He pondered this as he looked for any signs of others. Then he heard the shots.

First shot, and he counted off. At the five second mark, another shot. After what felt like a long wait, but was only another five seconds, a third shot rang out. Duncan looked around him and broke cover. The big pastor started hustling up the lane and through the traps in record speed. The timing of those shots was something universally taught in hunter safety to kids. It meant help. With no other gunshots, he assumed someone got hurt. He hurried as fast as his old out-of-shape body would let him.

Lisa saw him as he made it out of the tree line and into the main portion of the field leading up to the homestead. She sometimes had to bite her tongue about being left alone at the house, or in this situation. She was supposed to wait for one of the men to come get her. She understood why, but by the sound of the shots, it was one of her sons. She prayed everyone was okay while she loaded magazines for an old Beretta 9 mm into her back pocket and racked the slide to make sure she had a live round in it.

She used to shoot years ago with her late husband, and luck would have it that one of the guns the last set of raiders had been carrying was one of her favorites. She debated on taking a rifle with her, but didn't want to take the time to get it. She turned the safety on and tucked the pistol in her back waistband before she hurried to the hillside, staying in sight of the house, but moving closer to where she heard the shots from. Off in the distance, she heard two quads fire up, and she couldn't help but cross her fingers and hope that it was the Jacksons breaking off their honeymoon early, and not another set of raiders.

Relief swept through her body when she saw Duncan, red faced and running up the hill at a fast pace, his camo doing little to hide his bulk.

"Get one of the quads," he shouted to her when he was close enough for her to hear. She bolted to the barn.

There were five quads at the homestead, thanks to the first set of raiders donating three to the cause. The other two were still unfired, and they hadn't wanted to waste the precious fuel it took to run them. Lisa studied the controls for a minute and then turned the key. She forgot to choke it, so she fixed that and tried it and it fired right up. Luckily, it was an old Honda FourTrax, an automatic transmission four-wheel drive. Not much for speed compared to the other two, but big enough to carry her and Duncan.

She tore out of the barn, her hair blowing out behind her. Within seconds she was able to cross the large patch of grass between her and Duncan, and she put it in neutral and hopped off, letting the more experienced driver on.

"Hurry," she urged. "I think it was one of my boys."

"Don't worry. Hold on," he shouted as she tried to hold onto his waist.

They raced up the hill as fast as the machine would let them, and after a few minutes, they saw the two quads that Blake and Sandra used parked at the side of the woods on the northeast corner of the property. They parked next to the others, and Duncan hit the horn on the quad's handle. Then he shut down the vehicle. They got off the quad and noticed the dressed carcass of a deer nearby.

"Back here," they heard Blake shout.

Lisa tried to run ahead, but Duncan held her

back with a gentle hand and they walked together. She couldn't help but let out a sob when she saw her son's blood-covered face, the visible skin purpling from a bruise.

"Bobby, are you okay?" she asked him, noting that he was wobbly on his feet.

"Yeah Mom, 'tis just a flesh wound," he smiled wanly at her and tilted his head down and threw up.

"He's got a good concussion. We need to get him back to the house," Weston told them, handing Blake the rifle he had and then putting his brother's arm around his shoulders to help him walk it out.

The trip to the trail head was a somber one, the group pausing now and then for Bobby to vomit. Blake pulled the snares as they came out. He'd noted the dressed deer from earlier and realized that not only had the two been eager to learn, but they had a natural talent for placement. That alone would get them in the meat far more than having a perfect-looking snare. He did wonder about Bobby's injury. Weston had been tight-lipped about it, but once everyone got back to the cabin, they would discuss it.

"Who did this to you, baby?" Lisa asked him, the tears falling from her face.

"That boy and girl from yesterday. Mom, did I tell you she has the most amazing eyes ever?" Bobby babbled.

"He's scrambled," Weston said curtly before getting on the bigger Honda FourTrax.

They had Bobby slide on next, and then Lisa. She was almost sitting on the rear luggage rack, but was able to get on there and put her arms around Bobby. They'd quickly decided that because of size and weight, it had to be one of the girls, and Lisa immediately jumped on, not wanting her son to pass out and slide off as they climbed down the hill.

Duncan took the other quad, and Blake and Sandra doubled up. They made the slow journey back to the homestead.

CHAPTER 8

B obby kept slipping in and out of consciousness as the night went on. They laid clean towels behind his head and propped him up in the recliner in the main living room, putting his feet up so he wouldn't roll out. Lisa promised to stay by his side and make sure he didn't choke on his vomit, but they had to clean out the wound first. When he slipped into unconsciousness or sleep, Sandra shushed Lisa's protests and started cleaning out the ear.

The face wasn't much more than some scrapes and bruises, but his ear was badly injured. She cleaned the puncture out with precision. She poured half a bottle of hydrogen peroxide into a spray bottle and turned the nozzle into a stream. It was one of the many odd bits they'd found from the contents of the storage auction. She gently sprayed the ear down, wiping away the blood until the dried edges could be wiped clean. With a pair of tweezers, she removed bits of wood and bark that had punched through the cartilage.

"Dad? Blake?"

"Yeah?" Blake answered as both men broke off their conversation and approached the recliner.

Neither of them looked happy, and Duncan looked a bit pale.

"Do either of you have something we can stitch his ear up with?"

"How bad is it?" Duncan leaned closer to examine Bobby's ear.

"There's a hole. Looks like somebody brained him with a tree branch."

Duncan cursed softly. Lisa made soft murmurs while she sat on the floor beside her son.

"No, I don't have anything like that. I do have some superglue though," Blake said.

"That will work."

"I think I brought it in from the camper as I was moving my stuff inside here. Let me go look."

"Superglue?" Lisa asked, horrified.

"Yeah. It's almost the same thing as Dermabond. Super glue stinks worse and stings like hell, but he's out cold. He won't feel it."

"What kind of witch doctoring is this?" Weston asked, coming to join the conversation.

"They are going to superglue your brother's ear closed."

ASHES OF THE WORLD

"Oh that. Yeah, I've used that on cuts a few times."

"What? What do you mean—"

Her words were cut off as Blake produced the tube. With expert hands, Sandra pushed the flaps together to form a whole section of flesh in the upper part of his ear. Using a gloved finger on the back of the hole to support it, she managed to close the wound.

"What if she didn't get it all cleaned out?" Lisa was frantic.

"My first aid training went a little beyond the basics." Sandra's smile was meant to comfort Lisa, but the woman was overwhelmed, and all she could do was nod.

In no time at all, the ear was glued shut. They discussed whether or not they should wake up Bobby, but in the end they didn't. They would just have to watch him.

"There's something that's really bothering me," Blake said after they all washed up and cleaned around the armchair.

"What's that, hon?" Sandra put her arms around her husband, her face glowing from the contact.

"How did these two get behind us? I mean, they must have cut out through the woods and come up on the northeast edge of the property. The other thing…How many more of them are there? Are they alone?"

"I was worried about that too," Sandra admitted. "Worried that it was a diversion to get all of us out of the house so the homestead could be taken."

"That's a cheerful thought. What if it was just a simple honey trap?" Duncan asked.

"What's that?" Lisa said, moving closer to Duncan, wanting the same comfort he saw Sandra and Blake sharing.

He pulled her close with one beefy arm, his fingers gently rubbing her arm.

"Using a girl as bait, and then..."

"Sort of like what happened," Weston finished.

"Do we dare sleep tonight?" Blake asked everyone.

"I wouldn't, hon. We should set up watches all around. By Duncan's description, these kids were well fed and clean. I hate to say it, but that sounds like they have some sort of backup, or are being used for a trap, like Daddy said."

"I'll be honest, kids. That run up the hill tired me out. Would somebody else grab the watch by the lane?"

"I'll get it," Weston said.

"I'm going to poke around in the woods by where they came from. Maybe follow their back trail," Blake announced.

Sandra said, "I'll head out to go—"

"Hon, I need you to stay here with Bobby and Lisa," Blake cut in.

She turned on him, a look of anger on her face. Blake saw the fury in his wife's eyes.

"What?" he asked her.

"You're leaving me behind because I'm a woman?"

ASHES OF THE WORLD

The question rocked him. He hadn't meant anything of the kind and told her so.

"You're the one with the most current first aid, and you can take care of yourself and then some. I'm not asking you to stay back here because you're a woman, or my wife. I'm asking you because you're the best one for the job. If somebody were to try to take this place…"

"Okay, sorry. I thought it was some macho crap you were trying to pull." She looked at him, her expression softening.

"If they can come from us on the east side, they can find their way to the west. I'm going up to the barn to see if I can find a spot up top, one that's got a good view."

"Good thinking. Lisa, you going to be okay?"

"I've got to watch over my boy. If you could leave me a bucket in case he isn't done throwing up…"

"I've got stacks of them in the basement. We'll wash it out later if need be."

With a hug and a kiss, Blake and Sandra separated their embrace. Weston, Blake, and Duncan loaded up with guns, magazines, and water. Quickly and quietly, they headed out.

§ § §

Duncan's run up the hill had him worried. His chest was feeling funny, and he'd lost all his medication in the fire that consumed much of the countryside south of the highway. He'd honestly forgotten about it completely until his blood pressure surged upwards, making him queasy. When he was out of sight of the others, he pulled his pack off and searched through his small kit of medical supplies until he found a tin of aspirin. He chewed two of the bitter pills up and put things back before he went to the barn.

The structure overlooked the house; it would be an ideal spot for raiders to set up shop and pick off anyone who was holed up inside the house. From the second floor, they would have the advantage of seeing most of the valley. The only higher place on the property he found was where he set up Blake and Sandra by the old grain silo, but that was too far off.

He set his pack down inside the darkness of the barn and thought about things. What if the kids really were bait? Were they already under observation? He decided to look through the barn and grabbed a kerosene lantern instead of his flashlight, knowing the softer light from the flame wouldn't carry far. He lit it and quietly surveyed everything.

The lantern cast long shadows, and Duncan slowly crept through the structure, a pistol in one hand, the lantern in the other. When he felt secure, he headed to the corner where the smoker sat near the doorway to the root cellar. He descended the stairs slowly, memories of the gunfight that had happened down here threatening to overtake him.

He'd taken lives before, plenty in the war. Some

he felt bad about, others he didn't. His teachings in the Bible only made things more confusing at times, but no matter how guilty he made himself feel, he didn't feel bad about killing the man that had taken Lisa and Bobby. With a second knock on the head in such a short time period, Duncan was worried about Bobby. The kid should have woken up with all the fuss and his ear getting cleaned out, but he hadn't. He made a mental note to talk to his daughter later and pushed open the door to the root cellar.

He held the lantern up high to reduce the shadow and searched the room from head to toe. Potatoes, carrots, apples, and an area that one of the boys was starting to clean out. They wanted to move things around so they could start to store their canned goods and maybe move some of the cases of food down here and free up space in the house. He set the lantern down a moment to massage the sore spot on the left side of his chest. A tight band of pain squeezed his chest momentarily. His fingers went limp, and he dropped the pistol.

For a moment, he put both hands on the shelf to hold himself up, and he prayed. If this was going to be a heart attack that was going to take him, he wanted to see his daughter one more time. After a few moments, the band of pain started to dissipate, and his breathing came easier. He leaned over the empty potato bin and caught his breath, looking down the back side where his gun had fallen. No matter how far he reached down, he couldn't get to the gun. With a grunt he stood up and wiped the sweat off his brow.

"This sucks," he muttered to no one.

The entire bin was empty, but it was eight feet long and three feet deep. He knew it was going to be heavy, but when he pulled on one side, it moved. This surprised him, and he knelt down and peered under the bin. Old castors replaced the feet that were closest to the outside wall, and he pulled some more until the whole section was 90 degrees from where it had started. A clever set of hinges were exposed on the back side where the two bins were pushed together. Forgotten was the job of making sure the barn was secure. He felt a bolt of exhilaration and examined the wall behind it. Like the rest of the root cellar, the wall here was covered with rough sawn wood in various lengths. It was untreated and unremarkable, except for a peg that was sticking out about three inches near the floor.

Duncan pulled, twisted, and finally pushed the peg in. The section of the wall slowly shifted and swung away from Duncan and back from the floor. His heart rate was slowly climbing back up to dangerous levels, but he grabbed the lantern and then went back to the wall and gently pushed. A dark opening awaited his outstretched hand.

§ § §

Blake was moving through the woods as silently as he could. He'd put on some of his best camo and had traded out his deer rifle for an AR-15 with some extra magazines. The gun was lighter, the magazines held more ammunition, and even the ammo weighed less. That all meant he could load more firepower into an unknown situation. He wasn't sure if the smaller NATO round would drop a big boar hog, but he knew it would work on humans. He held the gun out in front of him at the ready and went to the gut pile where Weston had surprised him with the deer he'd snared.

He considered using a light, knowing he'd miss a lot less signs, but knew the illumination would give him away long before he could get close to the kids he was tracking. By moonlight alone, he was easily able to find his way back to the third snare set where Bobby was clubbed. The blood on the leaves and brush low to the ground looked black in the silvery light, and he soon found the tree he had marked earlier and started walking towards it slowly.

He had noticed this earlier, that somebody had dragged a deer from this point, the one Bobby was going to give to the kids. He moved slowly, not letting brush scrape against him, choosing his steps carefully. Moving slowly wasn't an easy thing for Blake. He wanted to rush ahead, find the kids and…That's where his plan went to hell. He knew he wasn't going to just shoot the kids from cover. He decided that it'd have to be improvised if and when he found them.

An hour into his slow journey, he found where

the ground had been scuffed and marred by many footprints. The leaves had been scraped aside to reveal the rich, dark loam of the forest floor. Then the trail seemed to stop suddenly. He hunkered down and studied the dirt, trying to make some sort of sense out of things. There wasn't enough light to see the exact shape of the footprints, but he was willing to bet there were multiple ones represented here.

Looking behind him and fixing his direction firmly in his mind, he looked around, letting everything in his vision go slightly out of focus. It was an old deer hunting trick. If you look for the shape of a deer, you usually will end up shooting a stump. If you look over everything and focus on nothing in general, your eyes will pick up movement and anything out of the ordinary. This is how he usually found what he was hunting—a flicker of an ear, the grass parting in a place where it all should have been standing tall, and sometimes nothing at all, because there was nothing to see.

A broken branch on a sapling caught his attention. It was about shoulder height on Blake, higher than an animal would have been able to reach. He watched around him, aware that he could be walking into a trap. He slowly approached it. A tuft of short brown hair stuck to the sharp edge of the snapped twig. It was hair from a deer. So from what he could tell, the kids met up with someone at this point, and two of them decided to carry the animal, rather than drag it. Smart, but there would still be a trail. It would be harder to follow in the dark, but now that he had a good visual starting point, he found he was able to still follow.

Little clues were found when it wasn't clear where the ground had been marred by feet. Snapped twigs, bark rubbed off the side of an oak tree from something that had brushed up against it, and other subtle signs. For another hour he slowly followed the trail, until the scent of cooking meat and wood smoke filled his nostrils. He didn't need the trail any longer. He followed the scent and was soon rewarded by the crackling sound and glow of a fire.

The trail stopped dead at the opening of a field of green alfalfa. A camp had been set up here, and it was far more than Blake wanted to bite off on his own, so he found a good spot to hide and watch. He could see at least ten men around the campfire, where large chunks of venison were spitted and being turned. Many of them were holding bottles of amber liquid, and crude torches were placed around the camp on long poles to provide a bit of light.

There were two older trucks, both hitched to trailers. One was what looked to be a bunkhouse-style camper, and the other was a flatbed trailer that had a tarp covering a boxy shape. The noise the men were making was loud and obnoxious, and many of them slurred their words as they drank and cussed. The camper's door slammed open, startling a few of the men, Blake included, and a crying woman was roughly shoved outside, followed by a man who was buckling his belt. He stepped off the trailer and grabbed her by the hair, pulling her to her feet and dragging her to the tarp-covered boxy shape. The woman disappeared inside.

Another man walked to it, reached in, and disappeared a moment, only to pull a new woman out. She screamed into the night as she was led into the camper. With the door closed, her screams increased, and it drove Blake crazy to sit still and not do anything. He expected to find the kids, or to find where they had gone, but he hadn't expected a large group. If he tried to intervene now, he would be dead, and his family wouldn't know what was going on, or what was to come. For the time being, he shut the noise out and concentrated on getting a good headcount.

Blake's small group, no matter how well armed, would probably die if they tried to assault this camp. Even clever traps or firing from cover would probably not work. Blake realized that the ten men he'd counted earlier were just the ones who were standing. He moved along the edge of the clearing, closer to the tarp-covered box, and saw another half dozen sleeping or passed out. He had no clue how many more were in the camper.

Soft sobs came from under the tarp, and he approached it from the camp's blind side and lifted the edge. The walls of the cage were made out of cattle panel, the top and sides put together with hog rings. The doorway was made by a square piece that was tied in place on one side, with a padlock closing the

ASHES OF THE WORLD

other. The smell of unwashed bodies hit him, and something shifted as he was staring into the eyes of a surprisingly clean-faced young woman. The description he'd gotten seemed to match Melissa, but he counted another seven forms in there.

"Please, don't hurt me. I don't want a turn," the young woman whispered, tears running down her face.

"I won't. Are you Melissa?" Blake matched her quiet whisper.

She nodded.

"I'm Blake; I'm the guy whose homestead you were just at earlier. Is your brother James in here?"

"No, James is in there." She nodded her head to the camper. "He isn't my brother."

"How many of them are there? The men?" Blake felt a knot of fear shoot through him as other shapes stirred and turned to look at him through the cage.

"Twenty-seven," a woman whispered, moving close to Melissa's side.

Blake reeled. This was worse than he thought.

"Are you going to kill me? I didn't mean for Bobby to get hurt. That was James, improvising."

"Why would you do this? To sucker us, to have us hurt? If you were free from the camp here, why didn't you run?"

"They have my parents, inside the camper. Along with the children."

"Children? Do they…?" His question sickened him, and he couldn't finish the thought. He knew what was happening to the women, but this added a new element, a new twist.

Nods from the dark figures made his heart hurt.

"Not all of them, and not the littlest ones," the woman who spoke to him earlier said. "Mostly the young ladies. Mostly. I'm Martha, one of the ladies who'd like to get out of here. Can you help?"

Blake nodded. The horror of the situation didn't stop Blake's mind from working, and he had a plan that was starting to form up.

"Is the group going to send more people to our place?"

"Yes. They are going to use another young set of kids. Either to beg or steal food. That will hold them over until the rest of them get here, and then they plan on taking your place."

"Taking it?"

"Yeah. They followed a set of trucks to your lane about a week ago and have been checking you out this whole time," Martha answered.

"How do you know all of this? If you're stuck in here."

"Pillow talk," Melissa answered, avoiding his gaze.

"Oh shit," Blake whispered. "I'm sorry, I've got an idea for getting you out, but I can't do it tonight."

"We've endured for weeks like this. One or two more turns won't kill me," Martha said, and the casual way she said it made Blake's guts twist.

"If these kids find or were given some food, how soon would those men eat it?"

ASHES OF THE WORLD

"Right away. They are almost out of food, and that's why they're planning on taking your home. If you were smart, you'd send the women away."

"I just might…But listen, whenever the kids come back with some food…don't eat it that night, okay?"

"You're going to poison them?"

"I don't know. We don't have as many people as this, so I have to do something. Make sure the kids don't eat either."

"I won't tell, mister," a muted voice from one of the forms said, and everyone echoed the sentiment.

"I promise I'll be back. Early morning after the kids bring the food back."

"Be safe." A hand reached through the panel, and Blake touched the palm and gave Martha a quick shake.

"Tell Bobby that I'm sorry," Melissa said softly.

"I will."

Blake belly crawled away, slipping into the woods unseen. He had a plan in mind, and it was a horrible one. He thought it would work, but it'd bring a horrible death, one he'd never wish on anyone until this day. All the components of the plan were already at the house, so he followed his way back to the homestead in the early morning hours, daylight starting to come over the horizon.

CHAPTER 9

Everyone was waiting at the house, with Blake being the last to arrive. The group looked weary, but Blake called everyone to attention and explained what he found, and what was coming. Not knowing when the big raid was taking place, they fell quiet, and he explained everything. They were just as horrified as he was, and when he told them his idea on how to take out a large force like that, he was expecting outrage and shock from everyone. Instead, he got a fierce nod from his wife and a vocal agreement from the rest.

"Then the following morning, we go in quietly and mop up," Sandra told everyone as the plan came together.

"We need more help, but can we feed all those women and children here?"

ASHES OF THE WORLD

"We can try, but remember, getting them out is one thing. There is still the other group coming. That's what I'm worried about."

"Do you think we can pull the same trick twice?"

"I doubt it. I think our best chance is to ambush the second group when it comes to that."

"Where are we going to put so many people?" Weston asked, having stayed silent during the briefing.

"Ladies and gentlemen, I'd like to show you something. Would you care to come with me to the barn?" Duncan asked, smiling for the first time, bowing with an exaggerated flourish.

"I'll stay behind. Somebody has to watch Bobby."

"Mom…" A weak voice croaked from the recliner, and everyone turned to see a bleary-eyed Bobby looking around.

"You're awake."

"Yeah. I was just tired. My ear feels funny." He was slowly touching the spot where his ear was mended.

"It's healing. You get some rest. I think we can leave him here for now and come look at Duncan's surprise."

They made their way to the barn, and the big man didn't say a word, but lit a lantern and headed into the root cellar. The potato bin was still rolled to the side.

"Watch this." Duncan broke the silence and pushed the peg in, and the section of the wall swung loose.

He pushed his way into the doorway and held it up so everyone could enter. The room easily was the size of the barn above it. Thick oaken beams and posts laid out every ten feet supported the structure on top. What stopped everyone dead was what was in the room. Row upon row of old rope beds lined one wall. What looked to be an earthen or clay trough twice as big as a bathtub was holding water.

Blake ran his hands through the water and smelled it. Not finding any chemical or stagnant smell, he shivered at the realization and looked around.

"Do you know what this place is?" Lisa was smiling broadly now.

"I think so."

"Oh, I know so. I found a diary." Duncan held up an oilskin-wrapped book, bound in leather.

"Your grandparents were part of the Underground Railroad?" Sandra asked, pulling her husband close and hugging him tight.

"No, but probably their grandparents, or whoever owned the land back then. I knew this place was old, but I had no idea..."

"It gets better." Duncan had started moving on, holding the lantern high to cast more light.

"This is seriously cool," Weston said, a grin on his face. "It's like a bunker, a hidden bunker. Did you know it was here?"

"No." Blake's voice was quiet.

ASHES OF THE WORLD

At the far end, where the barn should have ended, was a crude wooden door with a heavy bar. Duncan pulled the bar up and opened it, revealing a small room, and a small square tunnel that went off into the darkness.

"What is that?"

"A tunnel."

"Where does it go?"

"I er…uh…you know, I'm not sure I'd fit, and if I had to turn around…" Duncan stammered.

"This is amazing," Lisa beamed to Duncan and pulled him close, kissing him soundly.

Everyone looked elsewhere, and Weston made a couple of polite coughs after a few moments.

"Give me the lantern." Sandra took it from her Dad and knelt down.

She disappeared into the gloom, and even the light was swallowed up by it, it was so dark.

"Still okay, still okay," her voice floated back. They waited tense minutes.

"You guys wait there, I'll be out in a second. I want to check something out," she said.

"Okay, be safe," Duncan told the gloom.

"I should have gone in there with her," Blake told everyone.

"If you want to go, go?" Weston told him.

"Maybe I should."

"Surprise!" The shout from behind the group almost knocked everyone off their feet. Sandra had hung the lantern in the doorway to the root cellar and was panting hard.

"But how did you, you were just…"

"I'll have to show you. There's an old well that looks like it's boarded over…"

"An escape tunnel!" Weston almost shouted.

"Easy kid, you almost blew my ears out," Lisa said, her arms wrapped around the preacher.

"More than likely, an entrance. I don't know if this door can be opened from this side, can it?" Blake asked.

"Oh sure," Duncan said.

"You know, all the excess food in the house that's crowding everything…"

"Do you think its dry enough down here?"

"Yeah, it looks to be as dry as my basement. It has water—"

"And a toilet of sorts," Duncan told them, and they all turned to stare at him. "Come here, I'll show you."

They walked to the trough, and he pushed aside a rough wooden door to the left of it. Inside was an earthen construction.

"See, the artesian well that feeds the trough water has an overflow channel made out of this same clay. The continuously running water keeps it from becoming stagnant. It runs down through here and into this bowl."

They all stared at the crude toilet like it was the newest reincarnation of the computer age and marveled at it. Duncan held the lantern up so everyone could see the water coming in from the channel, swirling around and draining out the bottom like modern plumbing.

"But where does it go?"

"Probably through clay tiles or a crude septic system. This wall faces downhill, so it might just empty out in the hay somewhere…"

"This is really, really cool," Weston's enthusiasm was infectious, and Blake smiled back.

"We've been gone long enough. I'm heading back to check on Bobby," Lisa told them.

Everyone followed, but Weston was the last one out, rubbing his hands on the doorway before reluctantly letting the door swing shut, the weight of it allowing the locking mechanism to click. The wall became solid once again. They rolled the bin back into place and left the barn. They were still disturbed by what they were going to have to do, but their spirits were buoyed by the discovery. Everyone wanted to read the diary, but for now, they had way too much to do, and everyone was low on sleep.

§ § §

They rested for two days. They were refreshed and ready to go, but nothing happened. Bobby was up and on his feet, but he was still wobbly. He was able to take care of himself, if he moved slowly. The effects of the concussion lingered, but another week and he would be fine. As far as the plan went, they all had a bag of beans with them at all times. Mixed beans, and some smoked venison jerky, compliments of the Cayhill's snare.

The third day after nothing happened, Blake took the group of snares and set out to the north-eastern edge of the property line and set a string of them. He then set a string of the smaller snares along the edge of the woods for small game. For one of the last setups, he decided to build a spring snare. He was whittling the trigger piece when he heard someone approaching. He took his pack off and grabbed his rifle up. He backed away slowly, trying to be quiet.

"Hey, there's another one."

"This one's empty too."

"If we don't bring some food back, they said they were going to…"

Two girls stepped into view. Blake had called the younger Cayhills and Melissa kids, but these were girls. Maybe twelve years old. An ugly yellow bruise covered one cheek of the girl on the left. Most of her features were covered by a hoodie that was pulled tight. Blake considered what he had in his pack and then slid back into the tall grass of the hay, watching the edge of the woods until the kids discovered it.

They started pawing through it, looking over their shoulders nervously. They must have felt Blake's gaze, because they ended up finding the bags of food and then walking hurriedly into the woods. They were almost out of earshot when the girls spoke up just loudly enough for him to hear.

"Remember, don't eat any of this tonight."

ASHES OF THE WORLD

"Do you really believe they're coming to save us?"

"I have to. I don't want to have to start taking turns."

Blake waited until they were out of sight and retrieved his pack. He ghosted down the hill, wary that there were more people around. They had to start preparations for tonight or tomorrow morning. Now that they had a clock ticking, finishing things up was paramount.

CHAPTER 10

Over half of the food from the house had been moved into the barn's hidden dorms. Bobby eventually made his way down there and tried out one of the rope beds. He yelped when the old hemp stretched and then broke. Since no one was letting him help with the raid, he decided to busy himself down here, making sure things were ready for those getting rescued. He grabbed some rope from the hardware section of the Walmart truck they looted and started to replace the bed's ropes.

He marveled at how simple it was, the construction of it. Four posts, a box in the middle with holes drilled every four inches going across what would be the head and footboard, and more holes every six inches down the length. The rope was strung head to foot and back in one big continuous piece, then across the sides, woven over one row, under the next, over, and under, until a large net was formed. Just like a hammock. He finished his bed, tying a knot in the last piece. He tested it out, feeling it give, but satisfied to see that it held his weight. It felt a lot like a hammock, and he smiled at the comfort, jealous of the folks who were going to be staying here if everyone made it back.

He listened to Blake's plan and liked it, but had no idea if it would work. Because of his blog, he had spun off a YouTube video series where he would show different things in his gardening adventures, and one of the things he had been planning on doing this summer was using castor oil to scare off moles, voles, and mice. The heated oil could be used for dozens of remedies, including use as a laxative or something to make you throw up, birth control, and even wound dressings. He'd gotten a supply of beans for that purpose, and had been planning on using an old hand crank press his grandparents had owned, but the world crashed and burned, and the beans had sat, unremembered until now.

Everyone had started carrying a bag of mixed beans in their backpacks, as well as the jerky, and the plan was to give the kids food, or let them "steal it." Well, the kids had gotten Blake's bag, and he hoped the few pounds of beans would be enough to give his family and newfound friends the advantage they needed. The odds were grim, their numbers more than five times the size of their small homestead family, if you believed the information Blake got from Melissa. Once again Bobby thought of the message she had given Blake: "Tell Bobby I'm sorry."

He felt a sense of relief that she wasn't a willing participant. Because of the instant attraction he felt for her, he'd let his guard down and let James slip in behind him, only to be brained by a tree branch. He'd never been a believer of love at first sight, but there seemed to be a lot of it going around lately. He wondered if Melissa had also felt Cupid's arrow, but didn't dwell on it long. There was still a lot of work to do.

§ § §

The rest of the group was waiting, trying to go about the day as if everything were normal, but sneaking in rest when they could. They knew that it was going to be ugly and heartbreaking, and that none of them were guaranteed to make it back tonight. Sandra was beside herself when she thought of the way the women and children were being treated, and she wanted to head out just after dark. None of them knew how long it'd take the poison to kick in, so they compromised and decided to start their trek to the camp at 1 a.m. They would reach there by 3:30 a.m., where they would wait and see what was to come of things.

The walk through the woods loaded down with their gear was torturous and nerve-racking. Only

ASHES OF THE WORLD

Sandra and Blake seemed at home in the dark, so they took point. The trail between the two camps was becoming easy to find, and Lisa wasn't prepared to be able to pick it out, but she could. Too many feet had traveled back and forth in a short space of time. Lisa stayed close to Duncan, who held branches out of the way for her in the dark, with Weston bringing up the rear.

Bobby had been working in the basement shelter off and on all day, resting on one of the beds whenever he needed to. He had wished them luck, and lit a candle to lie down and get some rest. He was planning on helping the survivors settle in, if everything turned out.

§ § §

"Over there. I see one of them thrashing on the ground and others lying around the fire," Blake whispered.

"Are they dead?" Duncan asked.

"Can you smell it?" Sandra asked, and everyone nodded.

The air close to the camp smelled like an open latrine. They crouched lower when the camper door banged open and a man ran out with an armload of something. It banged into the bed of the truck where the caged women were being held.

"Do we wait?"

"I don't see anyone else," Weston answered.

"I'm moving in towards the truck, watch my

back," Sandra whispered.

She moved stealthily, her small frame casting almost no shadow in the dancing light of the main campfire. She could hear women and children crying the closer she got and could tell where the sounds were coming from. She lifted one end of the tarp and let it fall closed behind her. She saw several dark shapes and shining eyes looking at her thoughtfully.

"You are here to save us?"

"Yes. How many of them are dead?"

"Almost all of them. David is the only one who doesn't seem to be sick or dying."

"What about the people being held in the camper?"

"They are probably cuffed. They usually are always cuffed or chained."

"Are they okay?"

"They should be," the young woman answered.

"What can I do to help?" another woman asked as the sound of the camper door banged open again.

They all sat in silence, and when his footsteps got close, everyone winced. Sandra knew that Blake probably had the man in his sights, but they wanted to try to find one of them alive. It's not that they didn't believe the victims' stories here, but they wanted somebody who could tell them about the other group.

"Can you distract him? Get him to come over here?"

"You going to take him out yourself?" Melissa

ASHES OF THE WORLD

asked her.

"Probably. Looks like he has a knife and a pistol. I figured I'd brain him from behind, like what happened to one of ours."

She saw the stricken look on the young woman's face and connected the dots.

"Bobby is all right, and Blake gave him your apology, Melissa."

"Here he comes again," Martha said near the back of the cage where the door was.

Sandra willed herself to try to be invisible, to be as silent as she could be. She eased down so she didn't make a lump on the side of the trailer under the tarp.

"David, David!"

"Shut up, woman." The man's voice was hurried, cracked.

"You better let me out of here, or I'm going to hunt you down and hack your balls off."

"I'm not letting you out until I want a turn with you."

"You're the last one. Who says you're going to have any turns?" she snarled.

"Oh, so you think you can stop me?" The anger in his voice made it deepen, and Sandra could hear him moving closer to the door.

She let the tarp slide off her as she backed out slowly, pulling her pistol and knife.

"Yes I can. You always were the weak one. Charlie always said you were the biggest coward of the bunch. Why else do you think that you were always left behind to watch over us when they went out to raid?"

"Coward? You bitch, I'm going to carve you a new—"

Sandra sent the butt of the knife crashing down on the back of his head. It didn't knock him out, but he fell stunned, and she startled when she heard running footsteps. She swiveled and aimed her Beretta. Almost immediately she lowered it again, recognizing the forms of her friends and family. Blake fell upon David's form, and he used a length of bailing wire to secure him with his hands behind his back, the wire biting deep.

"How many more are there?" Blake growled into the man's ear.

"If Joe finally died, I'm the last one," David said.

"Duncan, Sandra, please mop up and be careful. Lisa, help me find the keys for this door. Shoot any of these men if they so much as move. They might be playing opossum."

"What do you want me to do?" Weston asked.

"If you don't mind, I'd like you to ask David some questions."

"Police procedure? Or how I've always wanted to ask a scumbag?"

"Totally up to you," he told Weston, who just smiled and cracked his knuckles before advancing on the now-cowering David.

"You came back for us," Martha told Blake, giving him a sardonic smile.

"I promised."

ASHES OF THE WORLD

"Who's the short-haired Tasmanian she-devil?"

"My wife, Sandra."

"Shoot. Why are all the good ones already taken?"

Her words made him crack up a little bit as he started examining the lock on the cage.

"The man with the black vest over there. He's got a set of keys," Melissa offered.

Blake left the cage and moved towards the man she'd indicated. The smell of loosened bowels and sickness hung over the corpse like a cloud. Not wanting to, but knowing it was necessary, he rolled the man onto his back and started searching his pockets. He came up with a lighter and jack knife in one pocket, and finally found the keys buried deeper than he'd like to have dug in the other pocket. He held them up, smiling. Lisa took the keys and started trying all of them while Blake went and inspected the bodies. The man who had been spasming earlier had now expired, and everyone else was dead. He touched each of them in the eyeball with his rifle before moving on, not wanting to get too close to them yet. He dreaded the cleanup and sorting through the rest of their belongings, but it had to be done, and done fast. No one knew when the rest of the group would be joining them.

The sound of flesh smacking flesh and sobs made him turn and run towards the camper, but he'd found Weston looming over a crouched David.

"Next Tuesday. They are getting re-supplied by the Guard unit and then moving on down here.

They can't break their orders until then," David blubbered.

"Guard unit?" Blake asked Weston.

"Yeah. Hey, take these," he handed Blake a set of keys. "It's for the truck he was loading up."

Blake wandered off, hoping he'd heard wrong. The truck fired up the first try and had half a tank of fuel. He shut it off and checked the bed of the truck. Camping supplies and guns. Lots and lots of guns. Most of it was military hardware of some sort.

"Don't kill him yet," Blake yelled over his shoulder. He watched Duncan and Sandra exit the camper.

"Baby?" Blake rose and started to run to his wife, who was carrying a small form that had wrapped its arms and legs around her torso.

They could all hear the kid crying, and Blake's heart broke. Sandra's eyes were moist with tears as well, and she tried lifting the child up to give to Blake to hold. The child made a piteous moan, so Sandra pulled him close again. The brief separation had shown him that it was a young boy, no more than five or six years of age.

"Is everything okay in there?" he asked her.

She just shook her head, fat tears running down her cheeks.

"One of them was still alive. One of the bad guys, I mean."

"Did you have to…?"

"No. The man was going to…hurt…little Chris here. He tried to hold him as a shield when he saw us. We'd already freed some of the men, and Dad had to uh…I'll tell you later."

The child's sobs were loud in the air, and a cheer went up behind him as Lisa got the door opened and the women streamed out. Following Duncan were over a dozen haggard survivors, older men and women, with a couple of children sticking close to their parents. Melissa ran to a bedraggled couple and hugged them fiercely.

It took the survivors some time to realize that they were free, and most of them took up the offer to come back to the homestead. Only one couple refused, thanking them, but not taking them up on it. The dorms were going to be filling up tonight, and they would be sorting things out in the morning. But for now, they had to pack things up here and bug out.

"Do we take the camper?" Duncan asked Sandra and Blake. "All the horrors that happened there…"

"I don't think so. I'd like to torch it personally, but we need to strip everything and get it back home."

"We can load up the caged trailer with stuff then, and have folks walk back?" Weston asked.

"I don't know if they can all walk or not. Not after what they've been through. Let's stage some of the gear in the camper. Then we'll have room in both trucks and the other trailer to drive them most of the way home," Sandra said.

"Okay, let's do that."

They worked furiously through the night until

dawn, packing everything up one way or another. One of their biggest finds was a working radio and some mobile handsets. Immediately their chances of survival went up with that one simple find. No longer would they have to wonder what was going on from afar. They could set things up for it to work, and Blake's solar setup could easily charge the batteries that ran the communications.

Moving the human cargo was not easy, nor was it fun. None of the women would ride in the caged trailer, and instead took the beds of the trucks. It didn't help that they were scared of all the men except for Blake. Those who would ride in the caged trailer were couples and kids. The camper was left behind, with some more guns and ammunition they simply didn't have room for. One thing they didn't find much of and quickly discarded was the food that the slavers had.

That's what this band had been about. Slaves. They captured men, women, and children, and had been selling off the men and boys for labor and the women as sexual slaves for sale or rent. In the two to three weeks that they'd been operating, they'd been traveling under a heavy convoy, some of it made up of former National Guardsmen. It was a chilling revelation, and even more scary for the fact that the country had fallen apart in a month's time.

"We can't let them get away with this," Sandra told her husband, who was driving the truck full of the women.

"We won't. It's part of the reason why I've got

ASHES OF THE WORLD

David stashed in the back of the second truck."

"Don't you worry that he'll get away and tell the others about our traps?"

"He's now the minority. He's in the middle of a camp full of folks who want him dead. The trick will be to keep him alive until the Guard makes contact again."

"Do you think…the world will ever be the same again?"

"I do. Out of the ashes, the phoenix rises." Blake's face was stone cold, looking at the trail ahead of him.

"Is that your fancy way of saying that the bad times are over?"

"No, not yet. But someday they will be. Things have to get better."

"Let's get these folks settled and then cook a huge feast."

"Sounds like a plan to me," Blake said.

"What about the little guy?" she asked him, a sleeping Chris on the bench seat between them.

"We'll figure it out."

"Besides, we have to finish our honeymoon." She poked him in the side and busted up when he jumped and let out a surprised squeak.

—THE END—

To be notified of new releases, please sign up for my mailing list at: http://eepurl.com/bghQb1

ABOUT THE AUTHOR

Boyd Craven III was born and raised in Michigan, an avid outdoors-man who's always loved to read and write from a young age. When he isn't working outside on the farm, or chasing a household of kids, he's sitting in his Lazy Boy, typing away.

http://www.boydcraven.com/
Facebook: https://www.facebook.com/boydcraven3
Email: boyd3@live.com
You can find the rest of Boyd's books on Amazon:
http://www.amazon.com/-/e/B00BANIQLG

Made in the USA
San Bernardino, CA
22 April 2016